Sticky Stuff

Written by Kate Walker
Illustrated by Craig Smith

An easy-to-read SOLO
for beginning readers

SOLOS

Southwood Books Limited
3-5 Islington High Street
London N1 9LQ

First published in Australia by Omnibus Books 2000

Published in the UK under licence from
Omnibus Books by
Southwood Books Limited, 2003

Reprinted 2004

Cover design by Lyn Mitchell

ISBN 1 903207 74 6

Printed in China

A CIP catalogue record for this book is available
from the British Library

For my dog, Jasmyne, who is always *stepping in chewing gum!* – K.W.

For Kip, Emily and Doug – C.S.

Chapter 1

Sophie set off happily for school one morning. She was winking at the sunbeams and smiling at the birds when, suddenly ...

Splosh! Squash! She stepped in chewing gum.

It was the *worst* kind of chewing gum.

Horrible yellow chewy!

Thick as pudding! Globby as glue!

Eeeee! Sophie tried to pull one foot out.

EEEEE! She tried harder to pull the other foot out.

But it wouldn't come.

She was stuck to the footpath, like a lid on a paint tin! Like an elephant in a vacuum cleaner! Stuck fast!

Chapter 2

Sophie's knees began to wobble.

Her stomach did flip-flops.

Most people caught in a fix like this would have yelled, *"Help!"* at the top of their lungs.

But not Sophie.

She looked at her feet.
Then she scratched her head.

Pretty soon she had an idea.

She reached down and undid one
shoe, and pulled that foot out.

She reached down and undid the other shoe, and pulled the other foot out.

And there she was!
Free as a bird!
Nothing to it!

Chapter 3

Sophie walked on, feeling very proud of herself. She smiled at the daisies and winked at the bees.

But then she saw that her brand-new socks were getting very dirty.

Dirty as dusters! Dirty as door-mats! In fact, *dirtier*!

Sophie stopped.
She scratched her head.
Then she saw just the thing –
a park bench.

She hurried over, sat down, and pulled off her socks. Problem solved!

But when she tried to stand up …

She was stuck.

Something had grabbed her.

Eeeee! She struggled and twisted.

EEEEE! She wriggled and squirmed.

Her backpack was stuck to the seat by chewing gum!

By globby green bubble gum – a monster patch! Its big round mouth had latched on and wouldn't let go!

Chapter 4

Sophie gasped!
   Her eyes went wide!
   Her curls stood on end!

Most people caught by a globby green monster would have screamed at the top of their lungs, *"Help!!!"*

But not Sophie.

She clenched her teeth and scratched her head.

In less than a minute she had an idea. A really clever idea!

She slipped her arms from her backpack.

She took everything out – her lunch, her pencil case, her books. And then she said, "Goodbye, old friend."

It wasn't easy to walk away and leave her dear old backpack behind. But Sophie did it. She marched on, brave as a soldier, and only looked back once.

Chapter 5

Suddenly, in the distance, Sophie heard *Clang! Clang! Clang!* It was the school bell ringing.

She was terribly late.

Sophie ran to the corner.

She wriggled under the fence.

She sprinted towards her classroom, and suddenly ...

Zinggggggg!

Back she came, soaring through the air like a bungee jumper!

Like a plane doing loop-the-loops!

Like a fly zapped by a lizard's tongue!

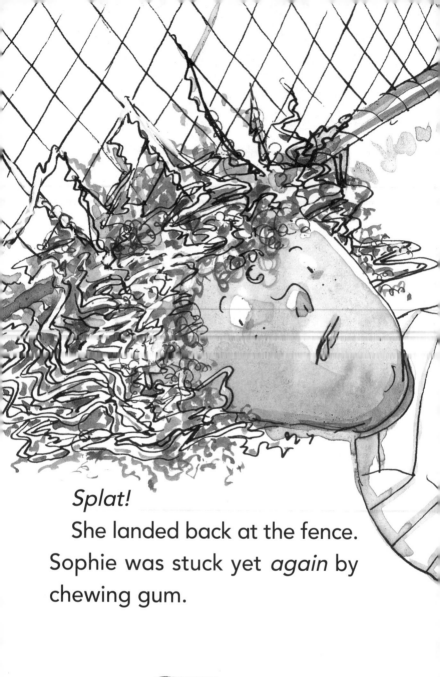

Splat!
She landed back at the fence.
Sophie was stuck yet *again* by
chewing gum.

SOPHIE

This time it was the *very worst* chewing gum in all the world. It was long, pink, stringy chewing gum, like hundreds of spaghetti strands!

It had grabbed every one of her curls!

Eeeee! Sophie tried to pull free.
But – YEEOOOWWW! – that really
hurt!

She had to stop.
What could she do?

She was sure that if she waited just a little while, a really clever idea would *zing* into her head!

She gave her head a little scratch to help the idea arrive.

Chapter 6

Just then, Sophie's teacher and her classmates spotted her through the classroom window.

They all came running. "Don't panic, Sophie!" they yelled. "We'll save you!"

They pushed and pulled!

And in no time *they* were all stuck to the fence as well. Stuck by their hair, their shirts, their headbands, their shoes!

They twisted and struggled!
They wriggled and squirmed!
But they only got stuck together worse than ever. They ended up like a lot of wriggling macaroni in stringy pink cheese.

Like most people caught in a
terrible fix, they yelled, *"Help!!!"* as
loudly as they could.

Meanwhile, the really clever idea Sophie had been waiting for *arrived*.

She stopped scratching her head and reached for her pencil case.

She zipped it open and pulled out …

… a little pair of scissors.

With a few careful snips, Sophie gave herself a very smart, very brave, very modern haircut.

And there she was, free as a butterfly!

Free as the breeze!

Chapter 7

Sophie was about to set everyone else free when a police officer arrived. She brought her car to a screeching halt, and jumped out.

Then a tow truck arrived.
Then an army convoy.

Then two fire engines …
an ambulance …
and a rescue helicopter.

39

Soon lots of people were working hard, trying to rescue the children and their teacher from the chewing gum.

They used ropes and ladders, saws and bolt-cutters, cherry-pickers and cranes.

And in ten minutes *they* were all stuck together as well! Stuck by their badges, their helmets, their gloves, their ponytails, their eyebrows, their beards!

All of them yelled at the top of
their lungs, "HELP!!!" And Sophie
knew exactly what to do.

Snip-snip! The teacher got a smart new haircut.

Snip! The tow truck driver got a shorter beard.

Snip! Snip! Snip! The children got interesting bits cut out of their uniforms.

The police officer lost her badges.
A fire-fighter lost his braces.
The poor helicopter pilot lost the
seat of his pants.

But everyone was happy to be free.

They raised Sophie on their shoulders and cheered.

From high in the air Sophie could see way over to the school gate. And there were all the parents, stuck in great blobs of sticky stuff!

Sophie scratched her head.

She would have stayed to rescue them ...

... but it was going home time.

Kate Walker

I was putting away my best teacup when – *crack!* – I bumped it, and the handle snapped off. I hated to see it broken. It had to be fixed – at once!

It took only one small drop of superglue to stick the handle back on the cup. And stick my fingers together. And stick my shirt sleeve to the arm of the chair.

I stood up quickly, bumped the table, and everything – pens, books and telephone – fell off! Everything except my best teacup. It was stuck to the top of the table. I thought: There could be a story in this!

Craig Smith

Sophie in this story is very happy to be going off to school. She doesn't let anything stop her!

When I was a child I *didn't* much like going to school. I lived near an army camp, and I thought it was more fun to watch the soldiers. I saw them running with all their gear, and jumping out of helicopters. It looked so exciting that I wanted to join the army myself.

I enjoyed illustrating the part of the story where the army comes to help. It brought back lots of memories. But now I'm glad I'm an illustrator and not a soldier!

More Solos!

Duck Down
Janeen Brian and Michael Johnson

The Monster Fish
Colin Theale and Craig Smith

The Sea Dog
Penny Matthews and Andrew Mclean

Elephant's Lunch
Kate Darling and Mitch Kane

Hot Stuff
Margaret Clark and Tom Jellett

Spike
Phil Cummings and David Cox

Lily and the Wiazrd Wackoo
Judy Fitzpatrick and Don Hatcher

Sticky Stuff
Kate Walker and Craig Smith